THE LAST KING
of
ANGKOR WAT

Graeme Base

Abrams Books for Young Readers, New York

**T**IGER, GIBBON, Water Buffalo, and Gecko sat among the ruins of ancient Angkor Wat.

They were looking at the old stone carvings of kings and parades, feasts and battles.

"I would have made a fine king," said Tiger. "I am so strong."

"Not so fine as I," said Gibbon. "If I were king, I would rule with compassion and kindness."

"I would be a ruler who never gave up, no matter what," said Water Buffalo.

"I would have been fearless in battle—I'm a great warrior!" said little Gecko, waving a twig like a sword.

They began to argue about who would have made the best king.

"I T TAKES many qualities to be a good king," came a voice. "Strength, compassion, resilience, and courage."

The animals looked around in surprise. They hadn't noticed the Elephant sitting amongst them.

"If any of you wish to know if you are worthy," said the Elephant, "go to the temple at the top of the hill."

They followed his gaze and saw an old ruin in the distance. None of them could remember having seen it before.

I SHALL win this race!" said Tiger, and he sprang away toward the distant hilltop with a mighty roar.

"Not if I get there first!" cried Gibbon. He leapt into the branches and gave chase, hooting as he went.

Water Buffalo snorted with determination and charged off through the jungle. "I shall never give up!"

"Wait for me!" cried brave little Gecko, and he scampered after them on his nimble feet.

TIGER BOUNDED through the jungle until he came to a swamp guarded by a fearsome Snake.

He stopped and snarled, muscles tensed and ready.

The huge reptile coiled itself to strike. Gathering all his strength, Tiger made a mighty leap over the Snake and raced on.

A LITTLE later, Tiger came across a Crane with a broken wing.

The bird called for help, but Tiger pretended not to hear—he needed to hurry if he was going to win the race.

GIBBON SWUNG through the trees until he too came across the Snake.

It seemed to be tangled in the branches.

"Let me help you," said Gibbon, untangling the patterned coils. Then he hurried off again toward the distant hilltop.

BUT AFTER a while, Gibbon became tired. He spied a giant Pangolin heading the same way and quietly lowered himself onto its back.

The Pangolin plodded on, unaware of its uninvited hitchhiker.

MEANWHILE, WATER Buffalo was pushing tirelessly through the jungle when she heard a voice.

"Do not be afraid," the Snake hissed. "You may pass."

But Water Buffalo trembled at the sight of the huge reptile and backed away, unable to conquer her fear.

DETERMINED TO finish the race, Water Buffalo trekked around the far edge of the swamp.

She plodded through an endless wilderness of twisted trees, until at last the end was in sight.

GECKO WAS scampering through the jungle when he found his way barred by the Snake.

But Gecko was not afraid. He dodged this way and that as the Snake tried to catch him.

"You're too slow for me!" he said with a laugh. And he scuttled off through the swamp.

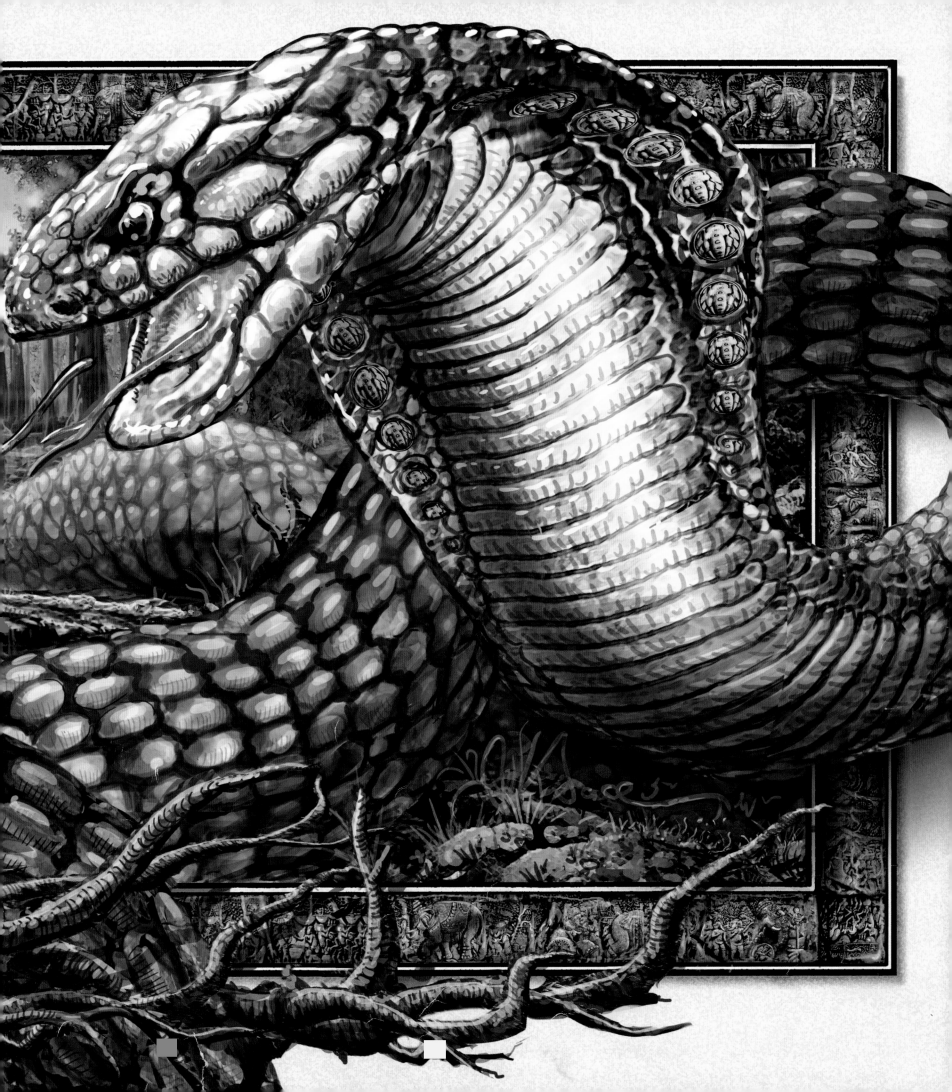

GECKO RAN on, leaping from one thick, twisting vine to the next—a handy path onward to the distant hilltop.

WHEN THE four animals finally arrived at the temple, they were astonished to find the Elephant waiting for them.

"Each of you has done well to reach the top of the hill," the Elephant said. "But let us see what your journeying has revealed."

"ONE AMONG you is clearly the mightiest," said the Elephant. "His strength enabled him to escape danger and reach the top of the hill first."

Tiger roared in triumph.

But the Elephant hadn't finished. "However, he ignored a call for help along the way. He lacks compassion."

Tiger looked away.

 NOTHER SHOWED kindness to a stranger," said the Elephant.

Gibbon nodded to himself.

But the Elephant hadn't finished. "However, he tired quickly and was happy to ride on the backs of others. He lacks resilience."

Gibbon hung his head.

"THERE WAS one who was determined and untiring," said the Elephant. "One who kept going until the end was reached."

Water Buffalo snorted with satisfaction.

But the Elephant hadn't finished. "However, she was unable to face her fear and was forced far from the path. She lacks courage."

Water Buffalo stopped snorting.

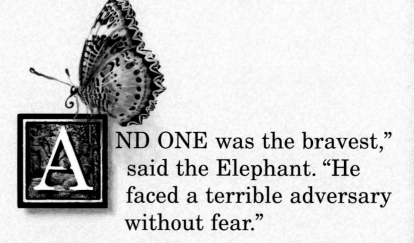

"AND ONE was the bravest," said the Elephant. "He faced a terrible adversary without fear."

Gecko chirped with glee.

But the Elephant hadn't finished. "However, he was foolhardy in the face of great peril. Even now he does not fully realize the danger he was in. He lacks wisdom."

Gecko chirped no more.

**T**HE FOUR animals went away to think about what the Elephant had said.

And there, at the top of the hill, they understood that none of them possessed all the qualities it took to be a great king.

WHEN THEY returned to the temple, they found themselves alone.

All around were fabulous carvings showing the life of an ancient Elephant King: scenes of strength, compassion, resilience, and courage.

TIGER, GIBBON, Water Buffalo, and Gecko went back down the hill.

As the years passed, the four animals became great friends.

Tiger grew more considerate. Gibbon stopped being lazy. Water Buffalo overcame her timidity. And Gecko learned to be less foolhardy.

None of them ever did become a great ruler, for those times had passed. But they never forgot the day they met the Last King of Angkor Wat.

The End

Angkor Wat is a real place in the north of the country now called Cambodia. The name means "City of Temples." Built hundreds of years ago by the Khmer people, it is part of a vast network of intricately carved stone buildings set in the middle of the jungle.

When the Khmer Empire eventually faded, the temples were abandoned, gradually disappearing beneath the creepers and vines. Now archaeologists are working to reveal the full extent of this ancient city, with new temples constantly being discovered. One particularly lovely area is called the Elephant Terrace…

How wonderful it would have been to see Angkor Wat in its original glory: a stunning city of temples surrounded by a lush jungle full of tigers, gibbons, water buffalo, and geckos!

Artwork created digitally on a Wacom Cintiq 24HD.

Cataloging-in-Publication Data has been applied for and
may be obtained from the Library of Congress.

ISBN: 978-1-4197-1354-5

Copyright © Doublebase Pty. Ltd, 2014
First published by Penguin Group (Australia), 2014

Printed and bound in China
10 9 8 7 6 5 4 3 2 1

ABRAMS
THE ART OF BOOKS SINCE 1949
115 West 18th Street
New York, NY 10011
www.abramsbooks.com